Text copyright © 2009 by Janet Russell
Illustrations copyright © 2009 by Jirina Marton
Published in Canada and the USA in 2009 by Groundwood Books

Groundwood Books / House of Anansi Press
110 Spadina Avenue, Suite 801, Toronto, Ontario M5V 2K4
or c/o Publishers Group West
1700 Fourth Street, Berkeley, CA 94710

We acknowledge for their financial support of our publishing program
the Canada Council for the Arts, the Government of Canada through the Book Publishing Industry
Development Program (BPIDP) and the Ontario Arts Council.

ONTARIO ARTS COUNCIL
CONSEIL DES ARTS DE L'ONTARIO

Library and Archives Canada Cataloguing in Publication
Russell, Janet
Bella's Tree / Janet Russell ; illustrations by Jirina Marton.
ISBN 978-0-88899-870-5
I. Marton, Jirina II. Title.
PS8635.U8745 B44 2009   jC813'.6   C2009-900468-2

Design by Michael Solomon
The illustrations were done in oil pastels on paper.
Printed and bound in China

For Violet Francis
(1910-2007)
Antonia
and
Bruno
— JR

To Katrina,
the most beautiful
girl I know

— JM

Bella's Tree

Janet Russell

•

PICTURES BY
Jirina Marton

GROUNDWOOD BOOKS
HOUSE OF ANANSI PRESS
TORONTO BERKELEY

BELLA, the girl, lived with her nan and Bruno, the famous dog, on top of a hill overlooking the sea. Bruno's fame came from bigness — not just bigness of body and bark but largeness of heart.

Nan was also famous.

For picking berries.

Nan could pick berries in the dark, she was that good at it and she loved it that much. But now she was old, and her berry-roaming days were slowing down. Where she used to pick far and wide, now she picked near and narrow.

But this was not the season for picking berries. It was the twenty-second day of December. Snow lay on the ground, around about and all around. All the berries that Nan had not picked that fall and the gulls had not eat were now under that snow, and that made Nan crooked.

"Are you crooked, Nan?"

"Yes, child."

"Why?"

"I can't stand the thought of all those berries under the snow. The frost is after gettin' them, and now there they are, gone. And that's not all. Christmas is soon here, and I haven't got it in me to go and get us a tree."

"I could get us a tree, Nan."

"Go on. Sure, you're not much bigger than an ax, let alone able to swing one."

"Not so, Nan. I am after gettin' big and strong and smart and well coordinated. You just wouldn't believe how big and strong and smart and well coordinated I am after gettin'."

"Don't worry your little head, Bella. Someone'll bring us a tree."

"But Nan, I want to get the tree. Please, please, let me get it. Tell me what to do and I'll do it perfect, I promise."

"Don't be foolish, girl. You're only a slip of a thing."

Outraged, Bella flipped onto her hands to show Nan just how well coordinated and unsliplike she was. Nan looked the other way and took up her knitting, pretending not to notice. Bella grabbed the knitting needles and purled up a palace.

For a minute Nan lost her tongue. When it came back she flapped, "Where'd you learn to do that?"

"Watching you," said Bella, a-twirling and a-purling tremendously pretty pattern work.

"Well, aren't you the well-coordinated little gadget. And here I was calling you a pup."

Bella could feel her advantage. For every argument Nan had, Bella knitted up a counter one. She almost had a sweater knit for someone bigger than anyone they knew, when Nan gave it up and went and got the ax.

"Good enough then," she said, handing it to Bella. "Go and get your nan a tree."

A smile smeared Bella's face. Nan sat down to unravel the sweater that was smart and strong and well coordinated but, when it came down to it, too big for anyone they knew. Bruno barked to get going, his large heart swelling with pride for Bella.

Off they went, Bella, the well-coordinated slip of a girl, carrying the ax just the way she'd been told to, and Bruno, the large bark with the swollen heart, hanging off her heels.

The twosome at onesome marched down the hill, over the snow-covered berries and into the woods. They came to a tree with a bird singing in it.

"Junco," Bella said, "we're out to get a tree for Nan for Christmas. Do you mind if I cut down yours?"

The junco was plain to look at but had a pretty song and was quite agreeable. "Welcome to it. As long as, that is, I can come and sing in it come Christmas Day."

Bella thanked the junco, chopped down the tree and dragged it home to Nan.

This, she thought, will straighten Nan right out.

"This is not a Christmas tree, Bella! This is an alder bush. Sure, it's not even an evergreen! Not a stitch of leaves on it! Naked! Or my name's not Nan."

Bella's face fell. Evidently, Nan was still crooked.

But even crooked, Nan was practical. She wasn't going to let no tree go to waste in her house. So she pulled out the box of Christmas tree decorations and dressed that naked little alder bush up like a — well, just like a Christmas tree. This straightened her out just enough to offer some advice on the topic of retrieving trees at Christmas.

"Bella, my trout. Here's a song to help you get a tree for your nan. As long as you sing it you'll remember that what we want is an evergreen and not another one of those naked little alder bushes or some other deciduous tree that's after losing its clothes for the winter."

EVERGREEN SONG
(to the tune of "Miss Mary Mack")

All trees have leaves,
but some leaves leave
their trees in fall
on the ground to sprawl.

All trees have leaves,
but the leaves that leave
from deciduous trees
can pile up to your knees.

All trees have leaves,
but some don't leave;
no, they don't go never,
they're evergreen forever.

The next day Bruno and Bella were off again, singing in search of an evergreen tree. This time they didn't stop until they came to a tree that was not a naked alder bush and not any other kind of an undressed deciduous tree, either. They stopped in front of a tree that was neither of those things, and in the tree was a chickadee.

"Chickadee," said Bella, "we're out to get an evergreen tree for Nan for Christmas. Do you mind if I cut down yours?"

The chickadee was plump and cute and chattered away that yes, yes, yes, of course it was — it was quite okay. Yes, please, by all means, take the tree — it was her plump pleasure to let them have it. Provided, that was, that the chickadee could come to their house on Christmas Day and chatter in it.

Bella thanked the chickadee, chopped down the tree and dragged it home to Nan.

This one, she thought, now this one will straighten Nan right out.

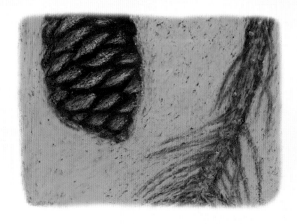

But no.

"This is not a Christmas tree, Bella! This is a spruce tree. And a spruce tree is no Christmas tree as far as I am concerned. Dear heart, child, what kind of a fool am I dependin' on the likes of you for a tree?"

Heaving out her crookedness lightened Nan's load. Her voice brightened a smidgen. It was less like the bottom of a bog and more like the whining and squeaking of an old door — still sorrowful but at least brighter than the bottom of a bog.

She carried on about the tree not being a Christmas tree for a little while longer, but crooked as Nan was, above all else she was also, in her own way, sensible. So after a decent amount of wailing and whining she set the spruce tree over by the alder bush and pulled out the box of Christmas tree decorations.

"Bella, girl. You need another song. One to know a spruce by."

SPRUCE TREE SONG
(to the tune of "This Old Man")

This old spruce, he had needles,
and all those needles had four sides each.
With a spin, twirl, give a whirl, in your fingers, girl;
all day long that spruce needle twirl.

This old spruce, he had cones,
and all those cones they did hang down.
With a spin, twirl, give a whirl, in your fingers, girl;
all day long that spruce needle twirl.

The next day Bruno and Bella set off again, over the snow-covered berries and through the woods, until they came to a tree with very long needles. They pinched off some of those needles and tried to twirl them. Not a whirl. All the while they were watched from above by two pine grosbeaks.

"Pine grosbeaks," Bella said. "We're out to get a tree for Nan for Christmas. Would you mind if we cut down yours?"

The pine grosbeaks looked at her for just less than the time it takes to scratch your nose, and then together they whistled that yes, it was, it was quite all right. Provided that was, that they could both come and whistle in their tree on Christmas Day.

So Bella thanked them, chopped down the tree and dragged it home to Nan.

This tree, she thought, is the one. Surely to goodness this tree will straighten Nan right out.

But no.

"This is not a Christmas tree, Bella! This is a pine tree. I should've known after the first two trees it was foolishness dependin' on the likes of you for a tree."

Nan mooed like an old cow about the tree not being a Christmas tree, but (remember now) crooked as she was, above all else Nan was, in her own way, sensible. So after heaving an appropriate amount of crookedness out of her, she set the pine tree over by the alder bush and the spruce tree and started in decorating it.

Nan turned to Bella. "You may as well give it up, girl. Tomorrow is Christmas Day and all the ornaments are used. Perhaps I don't deserve a real Christmas tree." And Nan looked downright sad.

"Nan," begged Bella, "just give me one last song and we'll get you a real Christmas tree. We can't stand to see you sad, Nan."

But Bella may as well have been talking to her nan's empty berry bucket hanging on the wall. Nan was sad and that was that. She didn't have it in her now to be singing songs.

Bruno could see the hole in Nan where the songs used to be and barked for Bella to give it up.

Off Bruno pulled Bella, down the hill, over the snow-covered berries, into the woods — past the alders, past the spruces, past the pines. They didn't stop until they got to a tree full to bursting with birds. Bella and Bruno looked at the tree and knew it for the perfect Christmas tree it was.

Kneeling down in the snow, Bella folded her hands and prayed to the flock of fluttering waxwings to let her have their tree for her nan.

"Waxwings," she sang, because she thought singing would be more convincing than talking, "oh waxwings, most beautiful and exotic cedar waxwings, please may we have your tree for my nan for Christmas?"

The waxwings froze. They just sat there, still as could be, sizing up that slip of a girl and her bark of a dog.

Quietly, to herself, so as to pass the time with patience, Bella began to sing. She sang each and every one of the songs her nan had pulled from behind buttons and given her. Just as she finished and was about to start them all again, the waxwings whistled back in that hissy voice of theirs that yes, she could, she could take their tree, but there was one condition. They would come on Christmas Day and sing in it.

Bella thanked the waxwings, cut down the tree and dragged it home to Nan.

It was late when they got home, and Nan had gone to bed. Bella and Bruno pulled the tree in and set it up beside the others. There were no decorations left. It stood there unadorned next to the tinseled alder, the bead-bedecked spruce and the shimmering ball-clad pine. When Bella turned out the lights, the new tree disappeared altogether.

The next morning, when Nan saw the tree, a smile cracked her crookedness.

It was a fir tree, and everyone knows that the fir tree makes the most perfect Christmas tree of all.

Bella threw open the window, and the birds flew in to sit in their trees — the junco in the alder, the chickadee in the spruce, the grosbeaks in the pine. The trees shone with their decorations, and Nan wished she hadn't squandered all the ornaments on the less-deserving trees that weren't after all, to her mind anyway, Christmas trees anyhow.

Her smile started to slack a slip. Before it slumped completely though, there was a whoosh through the window.

Fifty waxwings swooped in. They settled onto the fir tree and graced its every branch. They made that tree lovely, lovelier and more than loveliest.

Nan and Bella and Bruno and even the other birds lost their tongues to it. All the songs from the tips of the lost tongues tumbled onto their toes, and their eyes could not stop blinking for the beauty, the beautier, the beautiest.

And then Nan's Christmas tree began to sing.
And Nan's crookedness?
There it was.
Gone.